Big Tug

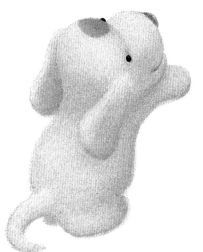

by Celeste White

illustrated by James Williamson

HOUGHTON MIFFLIN   BOSTON

"Here is a collar," said Mom.
Tug is too big for the collar.

Tug is too big for the mat.

"Here is a shirt," Mom said.
Tug can not pull it on.

Tug is too big for the shirt.

Tug is sad.

The collar, mat, and shirt do not fit.

What does Mom have for Tug?

"Here," she said.
"I have a big hug for you."

"Does it fit, Tug?" Mom said.
Tug is not too big for a hug.